Nipper the Noisy Puppy

"NIPPER!" The front door of the next-door house stood open. Inside, a man was shouting. "Nipper! Will you *please* be quiet!"

"Nipper?" said Ben. That's a funny name!"

"He must *nip* people!" Daniel pointed out. "You'll have to watch out, Adam!"

Adam tried to smile, but he was almost frozen to the spot with fear. *A dog next door?* And from the sound of the barking, it was a big fierce-looking dog with long, pointed teeth and a terrible growl . . .

Titles in Jenny Dale's PUPPY TALES™ series

Coming Next

More of Jenny Dale's PUPPY TALES
stories follow soon

All of Jenny Dale's PUPPY TALES books can
be ordered at your local bookshop or are
available by post from Book Service by Post
(tel: 01624 675137)

Nipper the Noisy Puppy

by Jenny Dale

Illustrated by Frank Rodgers

A Working Partners Book

MACMILLAN CHILDREN'S BOOKS

Special thanks to Narinder Dhami

First published 1999 by Macmillan Children's Books
a division of Macmillan Publishers Limited
25 Eccleston Place, London SW1W 9NF
Basingstoke and Oxford
www.macmillan.co.uk

Associated companies throughout the world

Created by Working Partners Limited
London W6 0QT

ISBN 0 330 37365 X

Copyright © Working Partners Limited 1999
Illustrations copyright © Frank Rodgers 1999

JENNY DALE'S PUPPY TALES is a trade mark
owned by Working Partners Ltd.

1 3 5 7 9 8 6 4 2

A CIP catalogue record for this book is available from
the British Library.

Typeset by SX Composing DTP, Rayleigh, Essex
Printed and bound in Great Britain by Mackays of Chatham plc, Kent

Chapter One

"Four-nil! Four-niiil!" Adam chanted as he acted out scoring the winning goal again.

Adam's mum, Mrs Roberts, was waiting at the school gates. "Hi, Mum!" Adam called. "We played Mr King's class at football this afternoon. They didn't stand a chance!"

"Adam scored two of the goals, Mrs Roberts," said Daniel.

"He was brilliant!" Ben added.

Daniel Carter and Ben Lewis were Adam's best friends. The three boys were always round at each other's houses, playing football. Ben and Daniel were going to Adam's for tea tonight.

Mrs Roberts smiled. "It sounds like you're a bit of a hero today, Adam."

Adam turned rather pink. He loved football and wanted to play for his favourite team when he grew up.

"I wish I was good at football," Ben grumbled as they all crossed the road. "I've never scored a goal in my life!"

"It might help if you didn't keep falling over your feet," Daniel pointed out.

Ben grinned and nodded. "Perhaps I'd be better in goal . . ."

But Adam wasn't listening to what Ben was saying. He'd suddenly noticed a man walking down the street towards them with a big Alsatian dog on a lead. Adam's heart began to pound and his knees felt like they'd turned to water.

Adam didn't like dogs. When he was four years old, a big bad-tempered old dog had snapped at him when he'd gone to stroke it. Adam had been terrified. He'd never forgotten it and had been scared of dogs ever since.

Ben and Daniel were still telling Mrs Roberts about the match, but Adam didn't join in. As the man and the dog came nearer, he slipped quickly behind his mum, out of the way. The Alsatian had big sharp teeth and a long pink tongue, and it looked a bit like the picture of the wolf in the story of Red Riding Hood which Adam's mum had read to him years ago.

The man and the dog went by, and Adam heaved a silent sigh of relief. Not even his mum knew just how much dogs frightened him, although she'd noticed that he didn't like them. Adam didn't want *anyone* to know – especially Daniel and Ben. They'd think he was a real wimp.

"Oh, Adam, I forgot to tell you," said his mum. "The new people are moving in next door today."

As they turned into their street, Adam saw a large lorry parked near their house. Men in overalls were hurrying in and out of the house next door, carrying chairs, tables, lamps and bookcases.

"Have you seen the new people?" Adam asked eagerly. "What are they like?" Their old neighbour, a pensioner called Mrs Miller, had been very nice, but Adam was hoping that someone he could play with might come and live next door.

"I've only said a quick hello," his mum replied. "They're called

10

the Taylors. They've got a baby and—"

"What an awful noise!" Ben interrupted, putting his hands over his ears as they got closer to the house and heard frantic barking.

"That dog is deafening! It sounds really fierce," Daniel added, doing the same.

"Ah, that's what I was going to say." Mrs Roberts smiled. "They've also got a rather noisy dog!"

"A . . . dog?" Adam repeated, in what he hoped was a normal-sounding voice.

"*Nipper!*" The front door of the next-door house stood open. Inside, a man was shouting at the top of his voice. "Nipper! Will you *please* be quiet!"

Ben and Daniel began to laugh. "Nipper?" said Ben. "That's a funny name!"

"He must *nip* people," Daniel pointed out, and they both laughed even harder. "You'll have to watch out, Adam!"

Adam tried to smile, but he was

almost frozen to the spot with fear. *A dog next door?* And from the sound of the barking, it was a big, fierce-looking dog with long, pointed teeth and a terrible growl . . .

Adam's heart thumped as his mum unlocked their front door. Every second he was expecting to see a huge, angry dog charge out of the Taylors' open front door and rush towards them, growling. Having a scary dog living next door was his worst nightmare. But this wasn't a dream. It was horribly real.

Chapter Two

The dog was even bigger and fiercer than Adam had imagined. It was jet-black and it had huge, fiery eyes and sharp white teeth.

"Go away!" Adam croaked in a scared voice. "Leave me alone!"

The dog didn't take any notice. It began to growl deep in its throat, drawing its lips back in a snarl. Then it ran straight towards Adam . . .

Adam gasped and sat bolt upright in bed. The sun was streaming through the curtains. He blinked a few times then sank back against his pillow. He'd been having a bad dream – a nightmare about Nipper, the dog who'd moved in next door.

Nipper was barking again now, and although Adam could only hear him faintly, it was still enough to make him shudder.

"Adam!" his mum called up the stairs. "Time to get up or you'll be late for school."

Adam leapt out of bed. He wasn't that keen on school usually, but at least there wouldn't be any frightening dogs there. He got washed and dressed quickly, then went downstairs.

"Isn't that dog ever going to stop making a noise? It's driving me crazy!" grumbled Adam's dad, who liked peace and quiet at breakfast time.

"Oh, he'll be all right when he settles in," Adam's mum replied.

"He's probably just barking at the milkman."

There was silence for a few minutes, then the barking started again.

"I suppose he's barking at the postman now!" snorted Mr Roberts.

"Or the paper boy," said Adam's mum. "Mr Taylor told me that Nipper's already a very good guard dog."

"Have you seen Nipper, Mum?" Adam asked in a small voice.

"No, not yet." Mrs Roberts glanced at him as if she'd guessed why he was asking. "But Mrs Taylor told me he's still just a puppy."

Adam wasn't convinced. Nipper didn't *sound* like a puppy. Then he began to feel even more alarmed. If Nipper was already scary as a puppy, what would he be like when he was fully grown?

"Time to go, Adam." Mrs Roberts went to get her coat. "Don't forget your bag. You've got judo club tonight after school, haven't you?"

Adam nodded. That meant he'd be late home – which was great, because then there would be less chance of him meeting Nipper.

"I'm sure Nipper's very friendly really, Adam," his mum said gently as they went outside. "After all, the Taylors have got a baby. They wouldn't be able to keep Nipper if he was a dangerous dog."

Adam didn't say anything. Nipper might be very friendly to the Taylors and their baby – but that didn't mean he was going to be friendly towards Adam!

In the Taylors' hall, Nipper was patrolling up and down behind the front door. He'd already had to see off three intruders this morning. Two of them had actually pushed things through the letter box!

Suddenly Nipper stiffened. What's that? he thought. He could hear sounds and strange voices nearby, and he could smell strange smells!

"Alert! Alert! Strangers approaching!" he barked, to the Taylors.

*

*"Rouurrouff . . . rrouu rrouu . . .
Rouuroufff!"*

Adam nearly leapt out of his
skin. He and his mum were just
coming out of their house. If his
mum hadn't been with him, he
would have dived back inside
and shut the door. Instead he ran
down the path, looking anxiously
over his shoulder to make sure
Nipper hadn't escaped.

"It's all right, Adam," said his
mum calmly. "I'm sure Nipper's
bark is worse than his bite."
"So has he bitten lots of people?"
Adam asked nervously. It was just
what he'd been scared of.

"No, silly, it means that just
because Nipper barks a lot, he
isn't necessarily going to bite

you!" his mum explained.
"Maybe we should go round and
meet him sometime . . ."

Adam didn't say anything.
There was *no way* he was going to
go into the Taylors' house and get
attacked by an angry dog! As far
as he was concerned, it would be
just fine if he never set eyes on
nasty Nipper . . .

*

The next day was Saturday. Daniel and Ben came over to do some football practice. They all went out into the back garden as usual, but Adam couldn't help feeling nervous. He'd heard Nipper barking loudly again last night *and* this morning. What if the Taylors let Nipper out into *their* back garden at the same time? Was there any way the dog could get at him?

Adam looked at the fence between the two gardens. It was really high. Nipper would have to be as big as a horse to jump over that! But what if the bushes in front of the fence were hiding a hole that Nipper could squeeze through? What if he tunnelled underneath? Adam checked the fence behind all the bushes. It seemed sturdy enough.

"Hey, Adam!" Ben called impatiently. "You're half asleep! Are we going to play footie or not?"

"Sorry." Adam ran to get his football from the garden shed.

"Adam, I'm just popping next door to see Mrs Taylor," Mrs Roberts called round the back door. "She wants to borrow a screwdriver."

"All right," Adam said. As long as she didn't want *him* to go next door!

Just then the telephone began to ring in the hall. "Oh, that's sure to be your gran, Adam," Mrs

Roberts said with a sigh. "And I really haven't got time to stop and chat either."

"We'll go next door for you, Mrs Roberts," Daniel offered politely.

Adam froze in shock.

"Well, thank you, Daniel," said Mrs Roberts, glancing at Adam. "But I don't want to spoil your game . . ."

"No problem," said Ben. "We don't mind, do we, Adam?"

Adam looked at Daniel and Ben. What could he do? If he said no, they'd want to know why . . .

"No," he muttered, "we don't mind at all."

Chapter Three

"Come on then," said Daniel, heading for the side gate that led round to the front of the houses.

"Do you think we might get to meet Noisy Nipper?" Ben laughed, as he followed.

"Just a minute," Adam said. His throat was so dry he could hardly get the words out. "Why don't you two stay here – sort out what we're going to use for goals?"

Adam couldn't go next door with Daniel and Ben. He just couldn't. What if he came face to face with Nipper and made a fool of himself in front of them? He'd never live it down . . .

Daniel shrugged. "Good idea – it'll save some time."

"OK, see you in a minute then," Ben said, kicking the ball to Daniel.

Adam went slowly through the gate and out into the street. He could hardly believe what he was about to do. But *anything* was better than looking stupid in front of his mates.

He paused by the Taylors' gate. Maybe he could just push the screwdriver through the letter box. Or leave it outside on the step. Nipper might even be out for a walk with Mr or Mrs Taylor, and then there wouldn't be a problem . . .

Nipper yawned and sprawled out more comfortably on the rug at the bottom of the stairs. It had quickly become his favourite place to sleep in the new house. It was the best place to keep an eye out for any intruders. If anyone came to the Taylors' front door, Nipper would know about it and immediately be on guard to see them off!

Suddenly Nipper pricked up his ears and growled softly. WAS THAT THE SOUND OF HIS FRONT GATE OPENING?

Adam walked slowly up the path to the Taylors' front door, telling himself there was nothing to be scared of. It didn't work, though, because he was shaking like a jelly.

Halfway up the path, Adam stopped. He thought he could hear a sort of clicking noise from inside the house. His heart racing, Adam listened hard. No, he must have imagined it . . .

Nipper trotted across the hall, his claws clicking on the polished wooden floorboards. He stopped by the front door and sniffed suspiciously. He could definitely smell a stranger on the other side. And the scent was getting stronger . . .

Adam forced himself to keep going until he finally made it to the Taylors' front door. There was still no sign of Nipper. Adam let out a huge sigh of relief. The dog must have been taken out for a walk, he decided, and, feeling much more cheerful, he reached out to ring the doorbell . . .

Chapter Four

*"ROURR ROURR . . . ROURR
ROURR . . . ROURR ROURR
ROUFFF!"*

Adam sprang back, tripped over
his feet and fell onto his bottom.
He got up again straight away,
glancing round to see if anyone
had noticed. But the street was

empty. He looked back at the front door, half expecting Nipper to knock it down flat and come charging towards him.

In the Taylors' hallway, Nipper scrabbled furiously at the door. "I know you're out there!" he barked. "Who are you? And what do you want with my family?"

Trembling, Adam looked around for the screwdriver, which had gone flying when he'd tripped. It was in a nearby flower bed, squashing a clump of marigolds.

He picked up the screwdriver and began to back away. He'd tell his mum that Mr and Mrs Taylor weren't in. It might be a fib, but that was better than coming face to face with an angry dog . . .

"Be quiet, Nipper!" Adam jumped as he heard Mrs Taylor's voice from behind the front door. So there *was* someone home.

"Hello?" Mrs Taylor called. "Could you wait for just a moment, please?"

Adam stood uncertainly, wondering what to do. He still

had a chance to get away before
Mrs Taylor opened the door and
the dreaded Nipper charged out,
baring his teeth!

Then another sound behind him
made him jump again. His
football had suddenly come flying
over the side gate, and
was bouncing into the Taylors'
front garden. The next second, the
gate opened and Daniel and Ben
ran through, chasing after the
ball.

"Ben was trying to show off his
skill – he made a right mess of it!"
Daniel said, running into the
Taylors' front garden. "What's up,
Adam? Aren't they in?"

"No," Adam muttered.

"Nipper's in, though, by the

sound of it!" Ben added with a grin.

Then, just as Adam reached the gate, the Taylors' front door opened.

"Oh, hello," called Mrs Taylor with a smile. "You must be Adam. Come in."

"Hello," Adam said weakly. Now he was well and truly trapped.

Daniel and Ben collected the football and went off to carry on with their game.

Adam braced himself, waiting for a large black, snarling animal to streak past Mrs Taylor and head straight for him. But nothing happened. Although Adam could still hear frantic barking, there was no sign of Nipper.

"Sorry I kept you waiting," Mrs Taylor went on, "but I had to shut Nipper in the kitchen. He's such a nuisance if he gets out."

Adam imagined Mrs Taylor dragging a large, growling dog down the hallway and into the kitchen. But he cheered up a little when he heard that Nipper had been shut away.

"LET ME OUT!" Nipper howled from behind the kitchen door. "I've got important things to be getting on with!" It was his duty to protect his family from danger. No one was allowed inside the house unless he'd personally checked them out first!

Then Nipper sniffed the air

suspiciously. The person who'd been standing OUTSIDE his house was now INSIDE! Nipper didn't like that AT ALL.

"Rouurrouff . . . rrouu rrouu . . . ROURROURROUFFF!"

"Oh, do be quiet, Nipper!" called Mrs Taylor. "It's so nice to meet you at last, Adam," she said, welcoming him in. She glanced at the screwdriver in his hand. "Is that for me? How wonderful – we seem to have lost the toolbox and so many things need fixing!"

"Yes." Adam handed over the screwdriver, peering uneasily down the hallway at the kitchen door. "My mum says you can keep it as long as you like—"

He was interrupted by a loud wail from upstairs.

"Oh dear, I thought the baby was fast asleep." Mrs Taylor sighed. "I suppose Nipper's barking woke him up! I won't be a moment, Adam."

She hurried up the stairs. Adam waited anxiously, his eyes still fixed on the kitchen door. Nipper had stopped barking now, but Adam could hear the dog sniffing and snuffling and scratching, which was just as scary!

"I've got to get out of here!" Nipper whined, doing his very best to pull the door open. "My family needs me!"

Adam blinked. For a moment
he'd thought . . . No, his eyes
must be playing tricks on him. He
thought he'd seen the kitchen
door move . . .

Adam told himself that not even
a big, strong dog could open a
door that had been closed. But as
he stared hard at the door, it
moved again! Adam's heart began

to beat so fast it banged against his ribs like a drum. Somehow the dog was managing to pull the kitchen door open. It hadn't been shut properly. Nipper would soon be free . . .

Chapter Five

The kitchen door was nudged open a couple of centimetres now.

Adam panicked. He ran over to the front door and tried to pull it open, but the lock was stiff and Adam's hands were shaking so much, he couldn't turn it. But he *had* to get away!

In desperation, Adam rushed up the stairs and onto the Taylors' landing.

"Adam?" Mrs Taylor came out of the baby's room, looking surprised. "What's the matter?"

Adam's teeth were chattering so much he could hardly speak. "Your dog's opened the kitchen door!" he gasped.

"Oh, I couldn't have closed it properly," Mrs Taylor said, shaking her head. "It has to be slammed shut really hard or it comes open again. There are so many things that need repairing in this house. It'll take us ages to fix them all—" Then she broke off and looked more closely at Adam. "Are you all right?"

"F-f-fine," Adam answered, trying to sound cool and calm.

"You're not scared of Nipper, are you?" Mrs Taylor raised her eyebrows. "I know he makes a terrible noise, but he's really very friendly."

Adam didn't look at all convinced.

"I'll tell you what, I'll go down

and let Nipper into the back garden," Mrs Taylor said kindly.

"I'm not scared of Nipper, really," Adam muttered, feeling very ashamed. He didn't like anyone knowing just how frightened he was of dogs.

"Well, I'll put Nipper out anyway," Mrs Taylor replied as she went downstairs. "Then at least the baby can get some sleep!"

Nipper had finally managed to get the kitchen door open. Panting hard, he dashed out into the hallway, sniffing every centimetre of it as he went. He knew that a stranger had passed that way, and he was determined to find out exactly who it was!

"Very interesting!" Nipper grow
softly to himself as he sniffed his way
over to the front door. "Whoever that
person is, he's still here – and I think
he's upstairs!"

Nipper headed for the stairs . . .

. . . only to be stopped in his
tracks by Mrs Taylor coming
down them.

"You bad boy, Nipper!" she
scolded, taking hold of his collar
firmly. "Now come along, I'm
going to put you in the back
garden for a while."

"But I don't want to go into the
garden!" Nipper barked sulkily. "I
want to protect you from the
intruder!"

"Now don't be silly, Nipper,"

Mrs Taylor said firmly. "You know you love going outside. You're just being a nuisance."

Mrs Taylor put him out and closed the back door.

"Let me in!" Nipper barked furiously.

"Thank you again for bringing the screwdriver round, Adam," Mrs Taylor said as Adam came cautiously down the stairs. "Say thank you to your mum for me, won't you?"

Adam nodded. "Nice to meet you," he said, hurrying over to the front door. He'd spent enough time with Nipper for one day!

"Oh no!" Mrs Taylor groaned as the baby started crying again overhead. "Can you let yourself out, Adam? Give the front door a good pull because it's a bit stiff."

"I know!" Adam said to himself as Mrs Taylor went upstairs again. He took hold of the lock and pulled hard, but it took him a moment or two to wrestle the door open.

*

Nipper had got bored waiting to be let back into the house. He was trotting round the garden, wondering whether he should dig up the juicy bone he'd buried in the flower bed the day he'd arrived in this new place.

"But if I do dig it up," Nipper growled suspiciously, "that person who's in my house might try to steal it!"

Nipper decided to leave the bone where it was. He could hear noises coming from the garden next door, and he could smell more strange people running around, although he couldn't see them because the fence was too high. They might want to steal his bone too!

Then Nipper pricked up his ears. He'd heard the sound of his family's

*front door closing! Nipper's tail
began to quiver and he dashed over to
the gate at the side of the house . . .*

Closing the Taylors' front door
behind him, Adam breathed a
sigh of relief. But his knees were
still shaking so much he wasn't
sure he'd be able to play football
now. He just hoped that Mrs

Taylor wouldn't say anything to his mum about what had happened—

CRACK!

Nipper hurled himself at the side gate. Part of the wood was rotten near the bottom and it cracked, leaving a hole . . .

"What was *that*?" Adam said. For a second, he thought Ben or Daniel must have kicked the football into the greenhouse and cracked a pane of glass. But the next moment, something came racing round the side of the Taylors' house and straight towards him!

Chapter Six

It was a dog! But it wasn't the fierce dog of Adam's nightmare. Adam stood rooted to the spot, staring at a plump little puppy.

This was Noisy Nipper?

"Hello there!" Nipper barked. "I need to find out if you're a friend or not!"

Adam swallowed hard. Was Nipper going to bite him? Adam wanted to call for help, but he couldn't get a single word out.

Holding his breath, Adam watched as the puppy circled round him, sniffing his football boots and ankles. With a patch of black fur over one eye, Nipper looked like a doggy pirate. The rest of his chunky little body was a soft, snowy white.

After a while, Nipper's short, stumpy tail began to wag a little. Adam remembered something his mum had once said: "If a dog wags its tail, it wants to make friends with you." Adam breathed out.

Nipper's tail began to wag

harder. "Yes, you seem to be all right," he barked. "In fact, I think we should be friends!" And he jumped up, putting his two front paws on Adam's knees.

Adam was so shocked, he almost fell over backwards.

"Aren't you going to say hello to me then?" Nipper barked. He stared up at Adam hopefully.

Adam still felt scared. But even though he didn't know much about dogs, he could see that Nipper was trying to be friendly.

"Hello, Nipper," he said in a shaky voice. Then he cautiously patted the top of the puppy's head.

Nipper immediately went mad with joy, barking and pawing

at Adam's knees.

Adam felt very nervous but proud of himself, although he couldn't help jumping when Nipper licked his hand!

"Nipper?" The Taylors' side gate suddenly opened and Mrs Taylor appeared. "Adam! Are you all right?" she asked, concerned, when she saw Nipper leaping

around him.

Adam nodded, still stroking the puppy. "I'm fine!" he said. And it was true. Looking down at the bundle of energy that was trying to lick his knees to death, Adam had to admit that Nipper wasn't nearly as scary as he had imagined.

"That gate's falling to pieces!" Mrs Taylor sighed. "No wonder Nipper managed to smash his way through it! Still," she said, smiling, "you two seem to have made friends now!"

"We certainly have!" Nipper barked happily. "I've checked him over and I think he's great!"

Adam still couldn't quite believe what had happened. He'd

been scared of dogs for so long –
and now here he was, making
friends with one!

"What kind of dog is Nipper?"
Adam asked as he bent down to
pat the puppy again.

"A bull terrier," Mrs Taylor
replied. "He's a real softie, despite
the terrible noise he makes.
Maybe you'd like to take him for
a walk sometimes, Adam? Oh,
and he likes playing football too."

"So do I!" Adam said. He
thought for a few seconds, then
made up his mind. "Er . . . do you
think Nipper would like to come
next door now and play football
with me and my friends?"

"I'm sure he would!" Mrs Taylor
bent down and ruffled Nipper's

ears. "Wouldn't you, boy?" she said.

Nipper licked her chin and barked in agreement.

A few minutes later Adam was walking into his back garden, with Nipper trotting beside him on his lead.

Adam was a bit nervous because he'd never walked a dog before and Nipper wasn't exactly very well trained. The puppy kept grabbing the lead in his mouth and shaking it from side to side, trying to pull it out of Adam's hand. He thought that was a great game.

Adam couldn't help laughing. He'd never realised before that dogs could be fun!

"Hey, who's this?" Daniel asked as he and Ben ran across the garden to meet them. "Is this Noisy Nipper?"

Ben knelt down and stroked the plump little puppy, who was clearly loving all the attention. "Hello, Nipper!"

"He's come to play football with us," Adam told them.

"Adam!" Mrs Roberts rushed out of the kitchen, her eyes wide. "That's a dog!"

"Yes, Mum, it's Nipper!" Adam said proudly. "I made friends with him when I went next door, and Mrs Taylor said I can take Nipper for walks and play with him whenever I want to."

Mrs Roberts looked as if she could hardly believe her ears. "Well, that's great, Adam," she said. "It looks like Nipper's very fond of you already!"

Even though Ben and Daniel were still fussing over the puppy, Nipper was pawing at Adam's leg, wanting Adam to stroke him. It made Adam feel really special.

"Come on, Nipper!" Adam ran for the ball and kicked it down the garden. "It's you and me against Dan and Ben!"

Nipper raced after Adam. "You're on!" he barked happily.

"I don't think I'll be so scared of dogs from now on. Some of them might be as nice as you!" Adam whispered as they ran down the

garden together. "And Mum was right – your bark *is* worse than your bite!"

Collect all of JENNY DALE'S PUPPY TALES!

The prices shown below are correct at the time of going to press. However, Macmillan Publishers reserve the right to show new retail prices on covers which may differ from those previously advertised.

All Macmillan titles can be ordered at your local bookshop
or are available by post from:

**Book Service by Post
PO Box 29, Douglas, Isle of Man IM99 1BQ**

Credit cards accepted. For details:
Telephone: 01624 675137
Fax: 01624 670923
E-mail: bookshop@enterprise.net

Free postage and packing in the UK.
Overseas customers: add £1 per book (paperback)
and £3 per book (hardback).